Little Royal

a fish tale

Chelo Manchego

SHAMBHALA
Boulder 2017

Shambhala Publications, Inc.
4720 Walnut Street
Boulder, Colorado 80301

www.shambhala.com

9 8 7 6 5 4 3 2 1

First Edition

Printed in China

♾ This edition is printed on acid-free paper
that meets the American National Standards
Institute Z39.48 Standard.

♻ Shambhala makes every effort to print on
recycled paper. For more information please visit
www.shambhala.com.

Distributed in the United States by
Penguin Random House LLC and in Canada
by Random House of Canada Ltd

Designed by Liz Quan

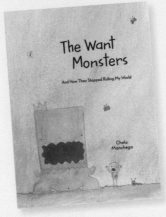

Also by
Chelo
Manchego

LIBRARY OF CONGRESS
CATALOGING-IN-PUBLICATION DATA

Names: Manchego, Chelo, author.

Title: Little royal: a fish tale / Chelo Manchego.

Description: First edition. | Boulder: Shambhala,
2017. | Summary: A very self-important fish
in a very small pond follows a frog to the biggest
pond of all, where a whale teaches him
important lessons.

Identifiers: LCCN 2016050557 |
ISBN 9781611804973 (hardcover: alk. paper)

Subjects: | CYAC: Fishes—Fiction. | Behavior—
Fiction.

Classification: LCC PZ7.1.M3633 Lit 2017 |
DDC [E]—dc23

LC record available at https://lccn.loc
.gov/2016050557

When I look up in the universe, I know I'm small, but I'm also big. I'm big because I'm connected to the universe, and the universe is connected to me.

– Neil deGrasse Tyson

I am the very big fish of my very little pond,

and when I demand, "Me! Now!" all of my very

little fishes bow down to me.

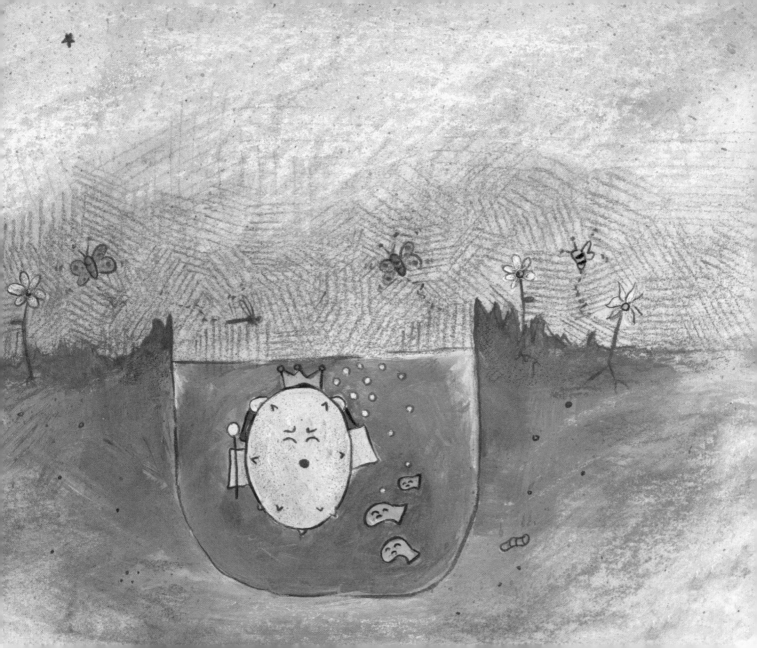

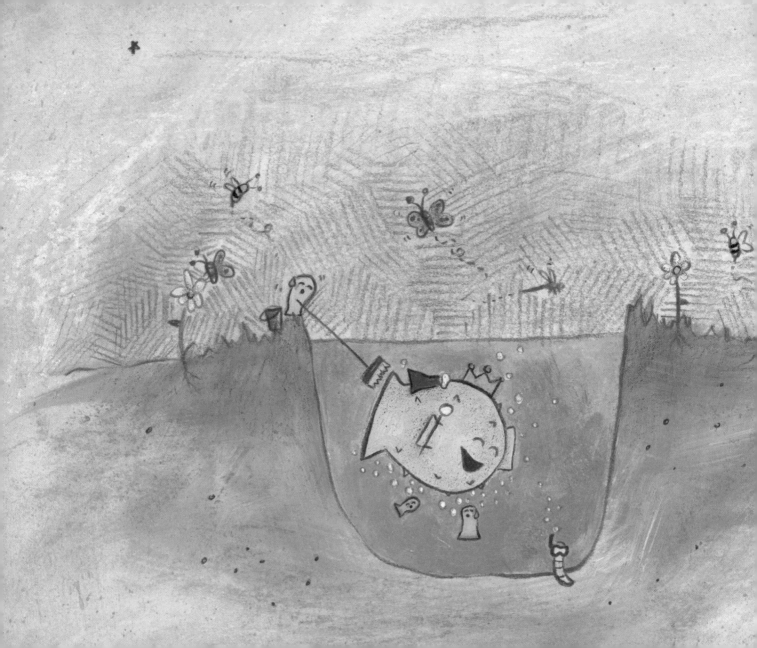

They scrub my tail and blow bubbles on my scales. So I chant, "Long live myself!" because I am the biggest and brightest, most beautiful fish in the kingdom of Me.

Then one day, something I have never seen before hops by. "You are very odd," I say. "I order you to tell me what you are!" The funny-looking creature laughs. "My! If you've never seen a frog, you must not get out much."

The truth is that I don't know what lies beyond this pond. But I lie, "I of course knew that, you fool! I was just testing you."

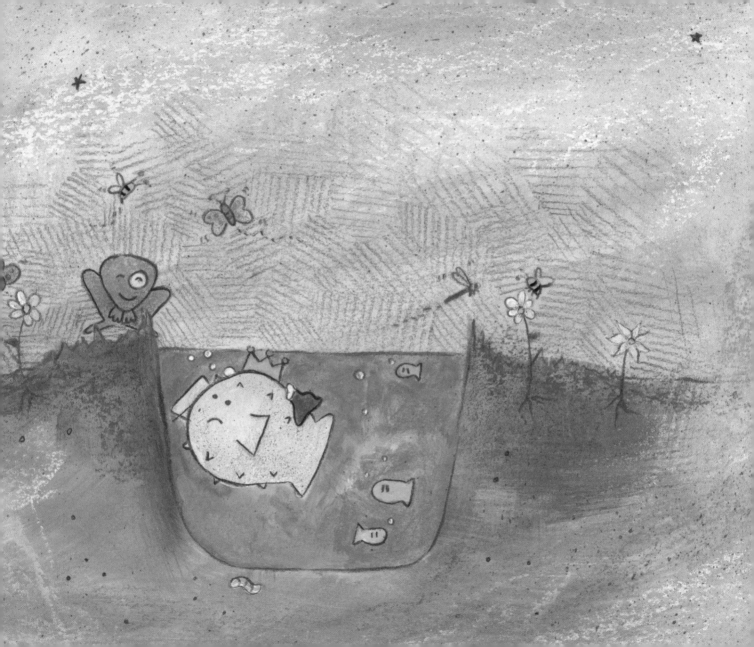

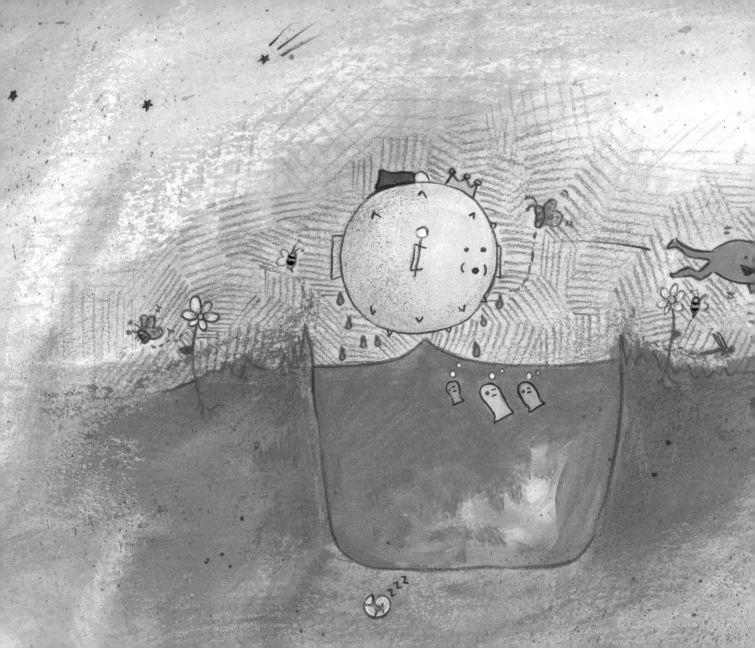

"I'd stay to chat, Your Majesty, but I'm in a rush to an even bigger pond. So, now if you'll excuse me, I must hop away," the frog says.

When I hear there are bigger ponds out there for me to conquer, my adventurous heart immediately fills up with curiosity and somehow—like magic—lifts me up to the quest. I leave my little fishes behind.

I land in waters where I am still a big fish in a little pond. "Surrender!" I order the fishes. And when I demand, "Me! Now!" all of the little fishes still bow down to me.

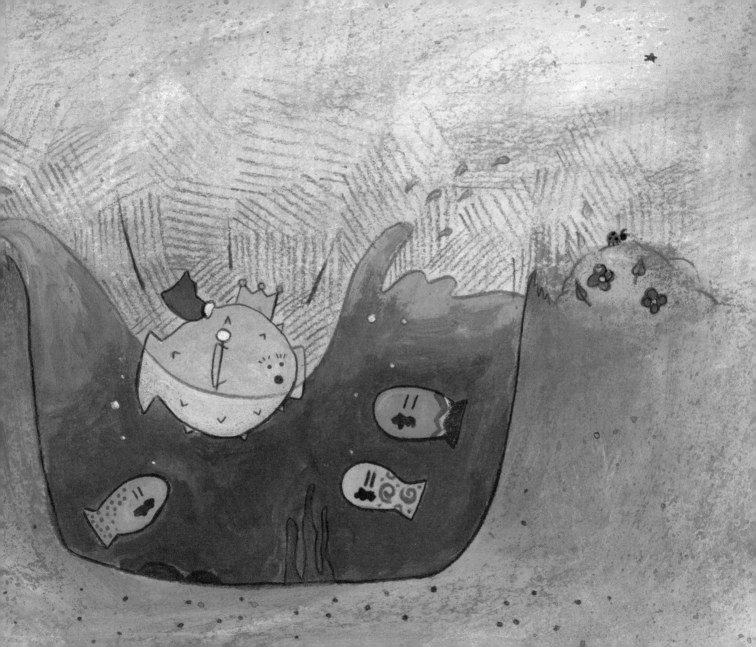

They still scrub my tail and blow bubbles
on my scales. So I chant, "Long live myself!"
because I am still the bestest fish in this
kingdom of Me.

But the frog keeps on hopping. "The pond
I'm going to is even bigger and more splendid
than this one, Your Majesty!" My heart again
immediately fills with curiosity and lifts me
up to the quest.

I land in waters where I am a medium-size fish in a medium-size pond. "Surrender!" I order the fishes, and when I demand, "Me! Now!" only some of the medium-size fishes bow down to me.

Only one scrubs my tail and nobody wants to blow bubbles on my scales. And when I chant "Long live myself!" the medium-size fishes giggle at me.

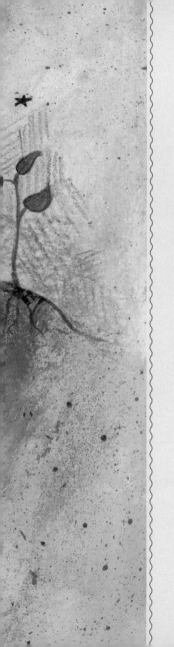

But the frog keeps on hopping. "Your Majesty, this is not it! The pond I'm going to is yet even more regal than this!" he says. And again my heart grows.

I land in waters where I am a small fish in a big pond. "Hmm . . . surrender," I whisper. When I demand, "Me! Now!" none of the big fishes bow down to me.

None of the big fishes scrub my tail, and I don't even mention blowing bubbles on my scales. So I chant quietly, "Long live myself," but nobody hears me.

The frog keeps on hopping. "Your Majesty, Your Majesty, we are so close to the *biggest* pond. I can see it!" I am desperate to go home, but my heart can't help itself and it lifts me to the adventure one last time.

When I land in the water, the frog says,
"They call it *Ocean*." I've never been so
terrified. "Look how big, how blue, how
beautiful. Isn't it magnificent?"

I see fishes of every color and every size.

Some swim fast and others slow. Some are

nice and some are not. Some don't look like

fish at all, and others look just like me.

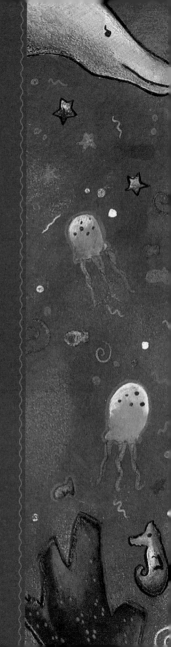

Then I see the biggest fish I've ever seen.
"Oh, please don't hurt me . . . Your Majesty!"
I yell. "I'll scrub your tail and also blow
bubbles on your scales, if you don't hurt me!"
In a very gentle voice it says to me, "Now why
would I hurt you? Besides, I don't have any
scales, you funny little fish. I am a whale.
You must not be from around here."

"You are the biggest fish—I mean *whale*—in this big pond. You can be the King and make the rest of us bow down to you!" The big eye looks at me intensely, but I see kindness in it.

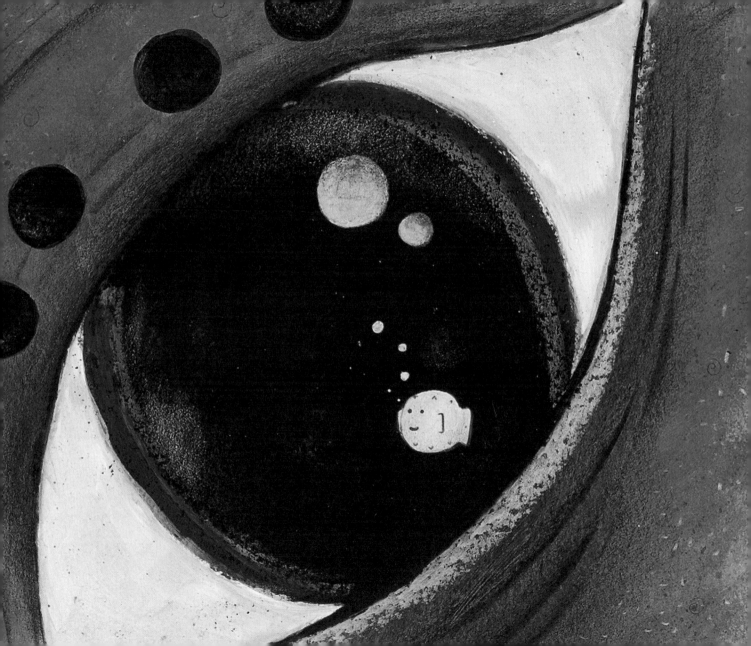

"That may be true. But you see, I also like to blow bubbles on my little fishes' scales and make them laugh. I doubt they'd want to come near me if I bothered them with such kingly demands."

"I might be the biggest whale in this pond, but there are creatures outside of these waters that make *me* afraid. They are actually small, but they are scarily astute hunters. Some are kind and pat me with their hands, but that's rare. So you see, my tiny friend, even I feel like a little whale sometimes."

My heart immediately feels sad. I cry so
much I can taste the water become saltier.
"I've been so terrible to my little fishes. How
cruel I've been! I wish I had made them laugh."
But my heart, in pain, can't lift me up
anymore.

With great tenderness, the whale says to me, "Come and sit on my back. Always keep in mind that you are inside a little big pond."

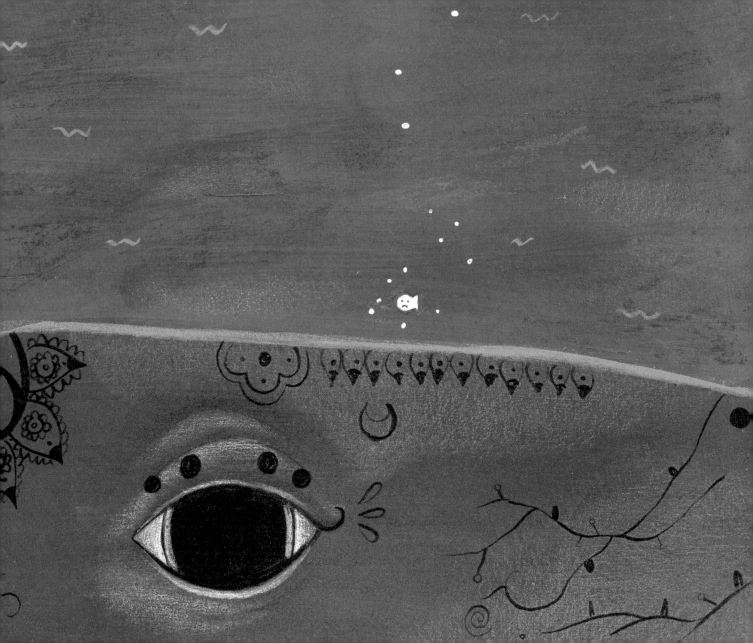

And before I can ask the whale what that means, I am shot up to the sky.

And up I go . . .

. . . And higher . . .

. . . And higher . . .

Until it gets so quiet I can hear my heart's wonder again, beating stronger than ever for what we have discovered.

Swimming in The Big Pond alongside planets and comets, with shooting stars, suns, moons, galaxies, and everything else around me,

I realize that I am a tiny drop of a very big, big ocean—a sublime ocean that I can enjoy when I go with its flow.

After a while, somehow—like magic—I float

back to my very tiny pond.

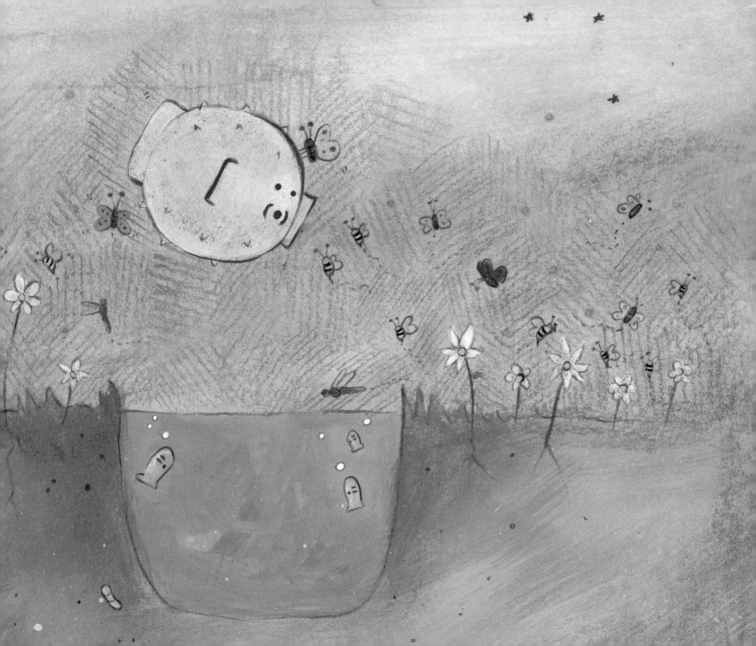

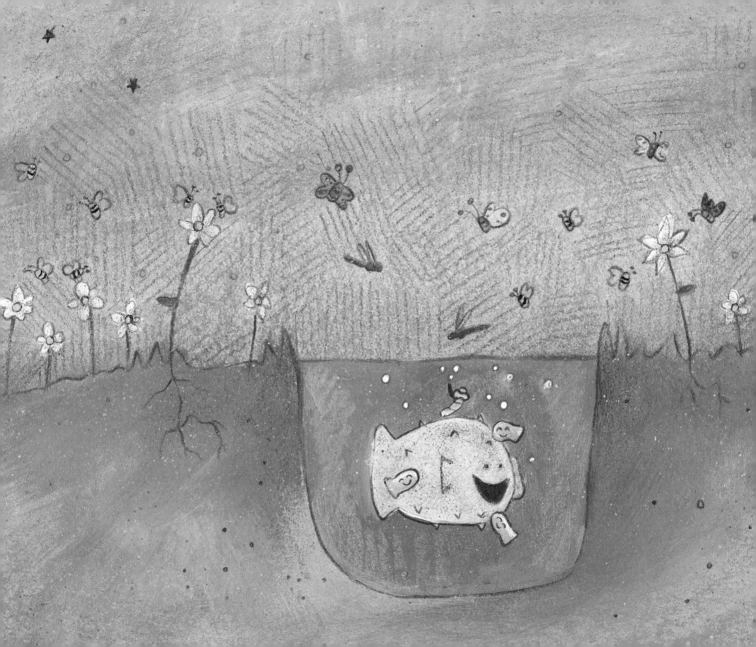

I become again a very big fish. But now
I think, "Others, all the time." I scrub their
tails and blow bubbles on my little fishes'
scales and I am happy that they are happy.

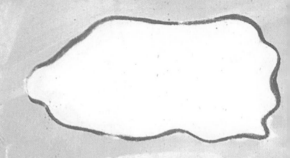

The End